THE TRIUMPHS OF FUZZY FOGTOP

THE TRIUMPHS
OF FUZZY FOGTOP

By Anne Rose ✳ Pictures by Tomie de Paola

The Dial Press/New York

to Gil, who knows the way to Chelm and back

Published by
The Dial Press
1 Dag Hammarskjold Plaza
New York, New York 10017

Text copyright © 1979 by Anne Rose
Pictures copyright © 1979 by Tomie de Paola
All rights reserved/Manufactured in the U.S.A.
First printing/Design by Jane Byers Bierhorst

Library of Congress Cataloging in Publication Data

Rose, Anne K.
The triumphs of Fuzzy Fogtop.

Summary / A fuzzy-brained but lovable man loses himself,
attempts to travel from Pinsk to Minsk, and mistakes the
identity of his old friend Harry.
[1. Humorous stories]   I. de Paola, Thomas Anthony.   II. Title.
P Z7.R7144Tr   [E]   78-72204
ISBN 0-8037-8646-8 / ISBN 0-8037-8647-6 lib. bdg.

The tales in this collection are based on stories of Chelm, which were told to the author in childhood. Chelm is a mythical town in Poland; its inhabitants are the traditional fools of Eastern European Jewish lore. There are other collections of stories about Chelm, different in detail. These differences simply reflect the mutability of an oral tradition.

Although the illustrations in the book are not meant to be strictly authentic, the artist studied photographs and paintings to familiarize himself with the village life of Eastern European Jews. Each line was drawn three times—first in ink, then in brown pencil, then in ink again—to get a feeling of depth and richness. The color was applied in watercolors and colored inks. Then the full-color artwork was camera-separated by the printer.

THE LIST

Fuzzy Fogtop was so absent-minded he forgot almost everything. In the morning he woke up remembering nothing from the night before.

"I'm in bed," he called to his wife in the kitchen.

"So you are," Fanny said.

"I can't find my clothes!" Fuzzy called back.

Fanny was tired of helping Fuzzy. She had been doing it for years. "Look for them yourself," she said.

Fuzzy looked here. Nothing. He looked there. Still nothing. He peered about the room for a long time.

Were those his socks, hanging halfway out the drawer? Was that his shirt, crumpled on the floor?

Fuzzy put his shirt and socks on, but the room felt drafty against his bare legs. His pants, where were they? And his shoes?

He pulled the blinds up so he could see better. There were his pants, dangling on the strings. And there were his shoes on the windowsill, smelling fresh as morning.

Dressed at last, Fuzzy went down for breakfast. "Here I am," he said.

"Do you know the time?" snarled Fanny.

Fuzzy patted his stomach. "I'm ready to eat, I know that."

"It's four in the afternoon," Fanny shouted. "The eggs are hard as stones, the toast is black as tar!"

"I like stone eggs," Fuzzy declared, "and tar toast only makes them taste better."

But Fanny had left the kitchen.

Fuzzy talked about his troubles with an old friend.

"Make a list each night," his friend told him. "Write down where your hat is, where your shoes are, your tie, your shirt, everything. Don't leave out a thing."

"A fine idea," said Fuzzy.

Before going to bed that night Fuzzy wrote on a long sheet of paper: "My hat is on the sofa. My shirt and jacket are in the closet. My pants are on the chair. My belt is on top of my pants. My socks are in my shoes, and my shoes are under the sofa." To close he added: "I'm in bed."

Then Fuzzy went to sleep.

In the morning Fuzzy felt a crumpled slip of paper in his hand.
"What luck," he said. "Now I'll know all I need to know."

He leaped out of bed and read the list. There were his clothes, just where it said they were. He slapped his hat on his head, pulled his socks and shoes on, slipped into his pants, buckled his belt, and threw his shirt and jacket on.

"Now I'll get breakfast on time," Fuzzy said.

He had come to the end of his list. But what was this? At the very bottom it said, "I'm in bed."

Fuzzy glanced at the bed. No one was on it. He whipped the covers back and turned as white as the sheets. No one was in it either.

"What's the use of finding my clothes if I'm lost?" he cried. "Where am I?" He sat down to think.

"I can't be far," he said. "I might be hiding in the closet." The closet was empty.

"I could have climbed out the window," he said. He leaned out to look but saw no one.

"Could I have fallen out of bed?" he cried. Crawling on his hands and knees under the bed, he stumbled against a forgotten old mirror. And there, in the mirror, was Fuzzy coming at him on all fours, right there under the bed!

Fuzzy was happy to have found himself again.
"No one could call me forgetful," he said.

FUZZY'S TRAVELS

Fuzzy was restless. He had never been outside his hometown of Pinsk, but now he was eager to try out the big world. He wanted to see the strange places he had heard about. He wanted to find out how people lived there, how they talked, what sorts of clothes they wore. In short, Fuzzy was ready to travel.

One morning he hitched his tired horse to a wooden cart and drove to the railroad station. He climbed onto a waiting train, found a seat, and sat down.

"What a marvel modern travel is," he said after a while. "At this rate I'll be there in no time and still feel fresh."

Dreaming and dozing in the train, he sat and sat. The longer he sat, the more wonderful the trip seemed to him. "How smooth this ride is," he said. "So smooth it doesn't even feel as if we're moving, but of course we are."

"This must be Minsk," he said after three hours had gone by. "I'll step outside and take a look at the strange new sights."

The first thing Fuzzy saw was a horse and cart very much like his own. "Remarkable how similar to ours these foreign wagons are," he said.

He walked on toward the center of Minsk. It looked very much like Pinsk. As a matter of fact some of the shops seemed familiar, but naturally they were not. They couldn't be.

He came to a street that resembled his own. The tailor shop was at the corner, just as in Pinsk, with the barbershop next door. Even the bakery was in the right place. Fuzzy could have sworn it was his own street, but obviously it was not. He knew it was not.

There must be many bakeries that look the same, Fuzzy thought. And tailor shops and barbershops as well. Still, Minsk looked a lot like Pinsk.

Strangers on the street greeted him warmly but Fuzzy did not talk to them. He was in Minsk, after all, not back in his hometown of Pinsk, where he knew everyone.

Having seen all he wanted to see, Fuzzy went back to his seat on the train and sat and sat. "What wondrous things trains are," he said. "Whether coming or going they seem to know the way."

After a time he peered out the train window again. There was his faithful old horse waiting for him. "Looks like I'm back," Fuzzy said.

His friends came to see him when he returned home from his travels.

"Did you see strange sights?" they asked Fuzzy.

"Everything I saw was strange. Minsk is like Pinsk, yet it isn't, if you know what I mean."

His friends nodded wisely.

"How do people dress in Minsk?" they wanted to know.

"People in Minsk dress the same as people in Pinsk, but somehow different."

"What are the houses like?"

"Houses in Minsk are small and close together, like houses in Pinsk, yet they're not the same."

"And the town itself, how does it look?"

"Minsk looks a lot like Pinsk," Fuzzy explained, "but the two are really nothing alike."

None of Fuzzy's friends had ever set foot outside of Pinsk. They didn't quite see how everything could be the same and also different, but they admired Fuzzy more than ever for knowing so much about the great big world out there.

HARRY

A man was sitting on a park bench reading a newspaper when Fuzzy Fogtop ran up to hug him.

"Harry," he cried. "It's good to see you, Harry!"

The man looked up at him in surprise.

"It's been a long time, Harry, I know," Fuzzy said. "How time flics."

Fuzzy looked closer at the man. "What happened to you, Harry?" he asked.

The man didn't answer.

"You used to be so handsome, Harry. Fat red neck, big hairy arms; what a man you were, Harry."

The man was silent.

Fuzzy shook his head. "The years haven't been kind to you, Harry. You're sickly looking now."

Still the man said nothing.

"What happened to that fresh pink face of yours?" Fuzzy asked. "It's green with age now. And that fine mustache, thick as a brush and shiny? A beauty of a mustache that was, and what do you have there now? A thin little line, sharp and mean."

The man folded his newspaper.

"Oh, you've changed, Harry. You have, no use denying it. That full head of hair, where has it gone? You're bald as an egg now, Harry."

The man stood up to go.

"Those merry eyes of yours, shrunk back into your head like dried raisins. What a change, Harry!" Fuzzy shook the man by the shoulders. "Harry, Harry, what happened to you, Harry?"

"I'm not Harry," the man said, walking away. "I'm John. John," he shouted. "John, you hear?"

Tears came to Fuzzy Fogtop's eyes now. "Were things so bad you had to change your name too, Harry?" he cried.